STEPHEN SAVAGE

SUPERTRUCK

SCHOLASTIC INC.

For my father-in-law, Bill,
who went everywhere in his super truck

ISBN 978-0-545-94498-4

12 11 10 9 8 7 6 5 4   17 18 19 20 21

Printed in the U.S.A.   40

First Scholastic printing, January 2016

The city
is full of
brave trucks.

The bucket truck fixes a power line.

The fire truck puts out a blaze.

The tow truck rescues a bus.

The garbage truck?
He just collects
the trash.

One evening,
it starts snowing.

It snows and snows and snows.

The city is caught in a terrible blizzard.

Just then, the garbage truck
sneaks into a garage and becomes ...

SUPERTRUCK!

He digs out the west side.
He digs out the east side.
He digs out the whole city.

Hurray for Supertruck!

The next morning, the trucks wonder about the mighty truck who saved them. Where could he be?

He's just collecting the trash.